The Mystery of the Dancing Angels

THREE COUSINS DETECTIVE CLUB®

#1 / The Mystery of the White Elephant
#2 / The Mystery of the Silent Nightingale
#3 / The Mystery of the Wrong Dog
#4 / The Mystery of the Dancing Angels
#5 / The Mystery of the Hobo's Message
#6 / The Mystery of the Magi's Treasure
#7 / The Mystery of the Haunted Lighthouse
#8 / The Mystery of the Dolphin Detective
#9 / The Mystery of the Eagle Feather
#10 / The Mystery of the Silly Goose
#11 / The Mystery of the Copycat Clown
#12 / The Mystery of the Honeybees' Secret
#13 / The Mystery of the Gingerbread House
#14 / The Mystery of the Zoo Camp
#15 / The Mystery of the Goldfish Pond
#16 / The Mystery of the Traveling Button
#17 / The Mystery of the Birthday Party
#18 / The Mystery of the Lost Island
#19 / The Mystery of the Wedding Cake
#20 / The Mystery of the Sand Castle
#21 / The Mystery of the Sock Monkeys
#22 / The Mystery of the African Gray
#23 / The Mystery of the Butterfly Garden
#24 / The Mystery of the Book Fair
#25 / The Mystery of the Coon Cat
#26 / The Mystery of the Runaway Scarecrow

99C

The Mystery of the Dancing Angels

Elspeth Campbell Murphy
Illustrated by Joe Nordstrom

BETHANY HOUSE PUBLISHERS
MINNEAPOLIS, MINNESOTA 55438

Mystery of the Dancing Angels
Copyright © 1995
Elspeth Campbell Murphy

Cover and story illustrations by Joe Nordstrom

Three Cousins Detective Club® and TCDC® are registered trademarks of Elspeth Campbell Murphy.

Published by Bethany House Publishers
A Ministry of Bethany Fellowship International
11400 Hampshire Avenue South
Minneapolis, Minnesota 55438
www.bethanyhouse.com

Printed in the United States of America by
Bethany Press International, Minneapolis, Minnesota 55438

Library of Congress Cataloging-in-Publication Data

Murphy, Elspeth Campbell.
The mystery of the dancing angels / Elspeth Campbell Murphy.
p. cm. — (The Three Cousins Detective Club® ; bk. 4)
Summary: The three cousins are stuck babysitting their bratty third-cousin Patience and when she disappears while they are visiting an old mansion, they must investigate.

[1. Mystery and detective stories. 2. Cousins—Fiction. 3. Christian life—Fiction.] I. Title. II. Series: Murphy, Elspeth Campbell. Three Cousins Detective Club® ; 4.
PZ7.M95316Myad 1994
[Fic]—dc20 94–49223
ISBN 1–55661–408–X CIP
AC

In loving memory of my father-in-law,
Howard R. Murphy,
whose life was filled with
love, joy, peace,
patience, kindness, goodness,
faithfulness, gentleness, and self-control.

ELSPETH CAMPBELL MURPHY has been a familiar name in Christian publishing for over fifteen years, with more than seventy-five books to her credit and sales reaching five million worldwide. She is the author of the best-selling series *David and I Talk to God* and *The Kids From Apple Street Church*, as well as the 1990 Gold Medallion winner *Do You See Me, God?* A graduate of Trinity College and Moody Bible Institute, Elspeth and her husband, Mike, make their home in Chicago, where she writes full time.

Contents

1

A Family Riddle

The way Sarah-Jane Cooper saw it, there was good-boring and bad-boring.

Bad-boring was when you got stuck doing something you didn't want to do.

Good-boring was when you had all the time in the world, but there was nothing you *had* to do. You could make plans if you wanted to. But you didn't have to.

If all you wanted to do was to lie on the grass and look up at the clouds, that was OK. In fact, this was one of Sarah-Jane's favorite things to do. She especially loved it when the clouds looked like angels. It always reminded her of a nursery rhyme her grandmother had taught her:

Grasp the clouds by will or chance,
And you shall see the angels dance.

Sarah-Jane loved the sound of that, but she had no idea what it meant. How could anyone grasp the clouds? Even if you could reach them, how could you hold on to them? And even if you could—why would that let you see dancing angels? It didn't make sense.

Sarah-Jane and her cousins Timothy Dawson and Titus McKay had once asked their grandmother what it meant. But all she knew was that she had learned it from *her* grandmother.

Grandma said the rhyme might be just pretty-sounding words that didn't mean anything. Or it could be a family riddle that would never be solved.

The cousins didn't like the idea of a riddle that would never be solved. They liked solving mysteries and finding things out. That's why they had a club called the Three Cousins Detective Club.

Sarah-Jane lay awake in the little bed in her grandmother's sewing room. Just taking her time getting up. Good-boring was waking up at your grandparents' house on a beautiful summer morning—the first day of your vacation there. Timothy and Titus were there, too. Timothy's baby sister, Priscilla, was too young to be away from her parents. But Titus had brought his Yorkshire terrier, Gubbio. Gubbio had never been there before and was very excited about having "grandparents" to spoil him.

The cousins' mothers, who were sisters, had told them a thousand times to be good and not to wear out Grandma's patience.

The cousins' grandmother, who was one of the most patient people in the world, had just laughed and said they'd be fine.

Sarah-Jane felt so grown-up and happy that she sang "Oh, What a Beautiful Morning" to herself as she got dressed.

On such a beautiful morning, what could possibly go wrong?

2

Visitors

When it came to their grandparents, the cousins were sort of spoiled and sort of not.

At least, that's how Sarah-Jane saw it.

Take breakfast, for example. Their grandmother would buy them any kind of cereal they wanted. But after breakfast, they had to rinse their own dishes and put them in the dishwasher.

Today they were extra spoiled. Donuts for breakfast! But there was also a note from their grandmother that put them on the honor system. Only two donuts each, and they had to have milk and juice, too.

They were on the honor system because their grandparents had already gone out.

Grandpa, who was a pastor, had gone to his

study in the church next door. That wasn't unusual. But it was kind of unusual for Grandma to be out so early.

She had left a note with the breakfast instructions. And at the bottom it said:

Will be back soon. Have gone to the train station to pick up Patience.

Grandpa always joked that Timothy woke up "bright-eyed and bushy-tailed." And that Titus "woke up slow."

Titus just blinked at the note. He said groggily, "I thought patience was something you got after all sorts of rotten stuff happened to you. So how can you pick up some patience at the train station?"

Timothy was already awake enough to think about it. "It's not *some* patience," he explained. "It's Patience with a capital P. That means it's somebody's name."

Titus blinked again. "Patience? That's somebody's name? Patience?"

"Patience can be a name," said Sarah-Jane. "In fact, there was somebody a long time ago in our family named that. I know because my mother told me she almost named *me* Patience."

At the thought of Sarah-Jane being named Patience, Timothy and Titus laughed so hard they almost fell on the floor.

Sarah-Jane would have gotten mad at them. But she could understand why it was so funny. She was *not* the most patient person in the world. Anyway, she liked being named after both her aunts—Timothy's mother, Sarah, and Titus's mother, Jane.

Sarah-Jane said sternly, "OK, so it's funny. But it's not *that* funny."

"Sorry, S-J," mumbled Timothy.

"Yeah, sorry, S-J," agreed Titus.

Sarah-Jane could tell they were about to burst out laughing again. But just then there was the sound of a car pulling up, and all three of them ran to the living room window.

Grandma and a lady about her same age got out of the front seat. Was this Patience?

Who was she, anyway?

The lady opened the back door and helped out a little girl. Sarah-Jane wasn't that good at guessing ages. But she thought the little girl looked smaller than a kindergartner.

She also looked a lot like Sarah-Jane. They both had red hair exactly the color of a shiny

new penny. Sarah-Jane didn't have a little sister. But if she had, this is probably what she would have looked like.

Timothy and Titus looked back and forth between the little girl and Sarah-Jane. "What's going on here?" muttered Timothy.

The cousins, feeling oddly shy, came out on the front porch.

The little girl didn't seem the least bit shy. She stood squarely in the middle of the sidewalk with her hands on her hips. First she looked the house over as if she were thinking of buying the place. Then she pointed at the cousins and demanded loudly, "Do they belong to me?"

3

Patience

To the cousins' amazement, their grandmother just laughed. This was puzzling, because—with *them*—Grandma was a stickler for politeness. And this kid was downright rude.

Even more surprising was Grandma's answer. "Well, yes, dear. I suppose they *do* belong to you."

To everyone Grandma said, "Let's all go inside and get introduced."

The cousins hung back a bit and went in after the others. Timothy muttered again, "What is going *on* here?"

"I don't know," replied Titus. "But I've got a bad feeling about this kid."

His little dog, Gubbio, seemed to agree. He made a funny whining noise—as if he just knew he was going to get his tail grabbed.

The cousins found the others in the kitchen. The ladies were having coffee. Grandpa had popped in to say hello. And the little redhead was scarfing down a donut. Gubbio took one look at her, made a beeline to Grandpa, and hid behind his feet.

"Now then," said Grandma happily. She rested her hand on the other lady's shoulder. "This is Patience. And she's my—"

"*I'm* Patience!" interrupted the little girl.

"Yes, darling," said the lady. "We're both named Patience. You were named after me. And I was named after *my* grandmother."

The cousins glanced at one another. So it seemed the little girl was the lady's granddaughter. But that still didn't explain who they were or what they were doing here.

But before anyone *could* explain, the little girl spoke up again. Loudly. "My name is Patience Elizabeth North. I live at 1535 Grand Avenue. My phone number is 555–1602. And I'm four years old."

It was on the tip of Sarah-Jane's tongue to say, "Who cares?" But from the way the grown-ups were beaming at Little Patience, she didn't think that would go over too well.

Grandma said, "It's wonderful how she knows her address and phone number."

Little Patience nodded as if she agreed that she had done something wonderful. She reached for another donut. The cousins watched her carefully. She'd better not try for more than two. . . .

Grandma Patience smiled fondly at her and looked over at the cousins. "You know, Grace," she said to their grandmother. "I just can't get over the resemblance between my Patience and your Sarah-Jane!"

"Isn't it something?" agreed Grandma. "You can certainly tell they're related!"

4

The Family Tree

***R**elated*? To *Patience*? Say it wasn't so!

But it was so, of course. Grandma Patience had even brought along a little chart to prove it.

"I didn't put *everyone* on our family tree," she explained. "That would get kind of confusing and take up too much room."

Grandpa, who was not going to be on Grandma's family tree, pretended to be mad and went back to work. Gubbio, who was not on the family tree either, trotted along at his heels. The cousins watched them go. So Gubbio had figured out how to get away from Little Patience. Lucky dog.

Grandma Patience said, "Let me show you how all the rest of us fit together. Family history—it's called genealogy—is a hobby of mine. I just love it! In fact, that's why I'm here today. Because of something I just learned about your great-great-great-grandfather, Daniel. I'll get to that in a minute."

She spread out the chart on the kitchen table, and the cousins bent to study it.

Grandma Patience said, "Your grandmother Grace and I are first cousins. Our children—my son, Tom, and your mothers—are second cousins. Our grandchildren—you

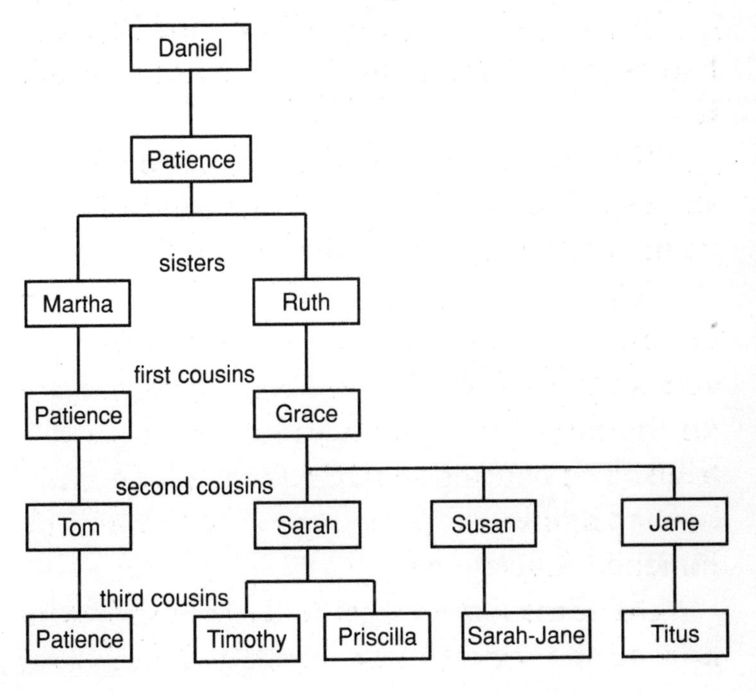

three and Patience—are third cousins."

So that was it. Patience was their third cousin.

"You mean . . ." Sarah-Jane spoke slowly, thinking it through. "That when Tim and Ti and I have children, our kids will be second cousins. And that when Tim and Ti and I have grandchildren, our grandchildren will be third cousins."

"Exactly," said Grandma Patience.

Titus pointed to the second name on the chart. "You were right, S-J. There was someone a long time ago in our family named Patience."

"I'M PATIENCE!"

"Yes, dear," said her grandmother. "But that was also the name of your great-great-grandmother. We can call her Long-ago Patience. That's how you and Timothy, Titus, and Sarah-Jane are related. You all have the same great-great-grandmother."

Maybe Patience didn't like the idea of that any more than the cousins did. Or maybe she just felt like being bratty. Whatever the reason, she waited until the grown-ups weren't looking. Then she turned to the cousins and stuck out her tongue.

Sarah-Jane hadn't done that in years and years. But Patience made her so mad she did it right back.

"Nonnie!" Patience wailed. "Sarah-Jane stuck her tongue out at me!"

5

The Woodcarver

The cousins' own grandmother looked startled—as if she couldn't quite believe what she had heard.

"She started it," Sarah-Jane mumbled.

Even though Timothy and Titus backed her up on that, Sarah-Jane felt her face grow hot. She knew what her grandmother must be thinking: A ten-year-old acting like a four-year-old.

No one expected what happened next.

Grandma Patience stuck out her tongue at Little Patience.

"Nonnie!" Patience gasped in a voice so shocked it made everyone laugh.

But her grandmother spoke seriously to her. "We've talked about this before, young lady. You don't like it when people do that to you, so you shouldn't do it to them. Now, where were we?"

"You were going to tell us about our great-great-great-grandfather," said Sarah-Jane, glad for a change of subject.

"Ah, yes!" said Grandma Patience. "Daniel was a master woodcarver. In a town not far from here, there's a beautiful 100-year-old house. It's being restored by the Historical Society. Well, in my research, I discovered that Daniel had worked on it! So I wrote to the historian in charge of the project. And what do you think! He invited us to come see the

house—even before it's open to the public. He said he can't wait to compare notes. And since it's so close to your grandmother, I just had to call her. We'll all go together. Isn't that wonderful?"

Sarah-Jane nodded politely. Who knew? It might be wonderful. Or it might be bad-boring. You never could tell.

"That must be such an interesting job," said Grandma. "Restoring old houses, I mean."

"Oh, absolutely," said Grandma Patience. "I even said that to the historian, Professor Brown. I said, 'If only old houses could talk. What stories they could tell.' And he said that he wished the house they're working on could tell them what happened to the ruby necklace."

The cousins perked up at that.

"What necklace?" asked Titus.

Grandma Patience explained. "There's a portrait of the first owners. And in it, the wife is wearing a beautiful ruby necklace that once belonged to a queen. The necklace should be in a museum."

"Why isn't it?" asked Timothy.

"Because no one knows where it is," said Grandma Patience. "It was never reported lost or stolen. It was never given away. It has never turned up anywhere. It's just gone. Professor Brown wonders if it could still be somewhere in the house. But, if so, they haven't found it."

"Aha!" cried Grandma with a laugh. "This sounds like a job for the T.C.D.C.!"

"What's a 'teesy-deesy'?" asked Grandma Patience.

"It's letters," explained Sarah-Jane. "Capital T. Capital C. Capital D. Capital C. It stands for the Three Cousins Detective Club. Tim and Ti and I are the only members."

It was at this point that Little Patience—who had been quietly watching her third cousins for a while—suddenly burst into noisy sobs.

6

A Little Name

"We didn't do anything!" cried Timothy, Titus, and Sarah-Jane all together.

"Sweetie, sweetie, what's the matter?" asked Grandma Patience.

It was a while before Patience could talk. And when she finally gulped out some words, they didn't make any sense.

"I want a little name! Nonnie, make them give me a little name!"

"Sweetie, Nonnie wants to make it all better. But she doesn't know what you mean."

Neither did anyone else.

Patience buried her head in her grandmother's shoulder. She settled down to just sniffles while her grandmother rocked her. "I want a little name," she mumbled to herself.

"She's had a big day already," said her grandmother. "Getting up early and riding on the train. Her grandfather and I are living at her house while her mommy and daddy are away. They got a wonderful chance to go to—"

"YURP!"

At first Sarah-Jane thought Patience had hiccupped. But then she realized she was trying to tell them something again.

"What did you say?" Sarah-Jane asked her.

"Yurp," repeated Patience. She seemed pleased that Sarah-Jane was still speaking to her after the whole tongue thing. "That's where my mommy and daddy went. To Yurp."

Sarah-Jane still didn't get it.

Then suddenly—she did.

"Oh, to *Europe*!"

"Very good, Sarah-Jane!" Grandma Patience smiled at her like one grown-up to another over the head of the little one. "Not everyone would have gotten that."

Sarah-Jane felt pretty pleased with herself. Talking to Patience was a lot like figuring out a riddle.

Grandma Patience said, "You know, I just realized that Long-ago Patience would have been about ten years old when the house her father worked on was built. She might even have gone there to see his work. So you three will enjoy it. Patience is a little too young, I'm afraid. But the chance to see the house came up so quickly, I couldn't get a sitter."

"Oh, don't worry about that," said Grandma. "Look how well Sarah-Jane understands Patience. Sarah-Jane and the boys will look after her."

Talk about mixed feelings. Here was Grandma, practically bragging about how grown-up Sarah-Jane was. Even after the whole tongue thing. That was good. But having to look after Patience? That was bad. Very, very bad. Boring. Bad-bad-boring.

7

Tall Tales

The cousins went out to the backyard for a breath of air.

Titus tipped an imaginary hat to Sarah-Jane. He said in an innocent drawl, "Well, now, ma'am. It looks like you're the one in charge around here."

"Yup," said Timothy. "We're just the hired hands. Around these parts they call us 'The Boys.' "

The cousins weren't supposed to say 'shut up.' But Sarah-Jane said it now anyway. She said it quietly, but with a lot of feeling. "Shut up, shut up, shut up!"

Timothy and Titus just laughed.

And Titus said in a whiny little voice, "Nonnie! Sarah-Jane said 'shut up!' "

Not even Sarah-Jane could keep from laughing then. But she still managed to sound fierce. "I mean it, you two. You'd better help me with that kid."

Timothy and Titus solemnly promised.

And just in time, too.

The screen door squeaked open and banged shut. Patience came running over to them.

"HEY, YOU GUYS!"

"Hey, Patience."

"Your grandma and Nonnie said you have to play with me."

"OK."

"And you know what? You're not supposed to let me get dirty for a few little whiles."

Titus and Timothy looked to Sarah-Jane for a translation.

"She means, we're leaving in a few minutes or a little while. And we're supposed to stay clean for when we go to the house, right?"

Patience nodded. "So what are we playing?"

Again Timothy and Titus looked to Sarah-Jane.

"We're going to spread a blanket on the

grass and look for shapes in the clouds," said Sarah-Jane. She used a voice that didn't allow for argument from anyone. In a way, she hated to use her favorite, private, good-boring thing to do. But she had to keep Patience clean and out of trouble for a few little whiles. And Patience seemed to like it.

After a while, Sarah-Jane relaxed a bit and said dreamily,

"Grasp the clouds by will or chance."

She half-expected Timothy or Titus to finish the riddle-rhyme.

The last thing she expected was to hear Patience say,

"And you shall see the angels dance."

The cousins sat up straight and stared at Patience.

"How did you know that rhyme?" Sarah-Jane asked her.

Patience shrugged. "My Nonnie teached me. How can you touch the clouds?"

"You can't really," said Sarah-Jane.

"I can."

"No, you can't."

"Yes, I can! Because you know how? That boy in the story is a *giant* boy. And he picked me up. And I was way up high. And I grabbed the clouds."

"What boy in the story?" asked Titus.

"Will."

"Oh!" cried Sarah-Jane, suddenly understanding. "Will is not a boy." When Patience started to protest, Sarah-Jane went on quickly. "Your *will* is when you *want* to do something. When the rhyme says, 'Grasp the clouds by will,' it means on purpose. When it says 'by chance,' it means you grasp them by accident."

Sarah-Jane was feeling pretty pleased with the way she had explained all that.

Patience nodded thoughtfully. "That's what Will says, too. He told me to pull on the clouds. And the angels danced. I danced with them. But Will didn't want to. Because you know why? He's a giant and when he dances everything shakes. He breaks things."

"Patience," said Timothy. "That is a tall tale."

"It is *not*!" cried Patience. "What's a tall tale? I don't have a long tail. I'm telling!"

And before anyone could stop her, Patience was up and running toward the house.

Sarah-Jane covered her face with her hands

and flopped back on the blanket. "Ohhh," she groaned. "Where will it all end?"

"It's going to be a long day," agreed Timothy.

"Come on," sighed Titus. "Let's go explain what really happened. Again."

Just then Grandma called cheerfully from behind the screen door. "Timothy! Titus! Sarah-Jane! Patience! Come on, kids! It's time to go."

The cousins struggled to their feet and folded up the blanket.

Then the same thought seemed to strike each of them at the same time. If Patience had gone inside to tell on them, why was Grandma calling her?

8

Hiding

"Oh, no!" cried Sarah-Jane. "We were supposed to be watching her, and now she's gone!"

"She can't have gotten far," said Titus. "Let's just think a minute. She didn't go in the back door or Grandma would have seen her. So she's probably somewhere in the yard."

"Or maybe she snuck around to the front and went in the house that way," said Timothy. "Or maybe she went in the church."

"Or maybe she wandered off," said Sarah-Jane. She couldn't keep the fear out of her voice. "Oh, please tell me she didn't wander off!"

At that moment, Grandma came to the door again to see what was taking them so long. The cousins ran over to the back porch. Grandma took one look at their faces and said, "What's wrong? Where's Patience?"

"She said she was going in the house," said Timothy. "A couple of minutes ago."

"We didn't actually *see* her go in the house, though," said Titus.

"Patience!" called Sarah-Jane. "Patience, where are you?"

Something crawled out from behind the big bush by the back porch.

It grabbed Sarah-Jane's ankle.

Sarah-Jane knew perfectly well that there were no boa constrictors in her grandparents' backyard. But to her shattered nerves, that's just what it felt like.

She screamed and tried to kick whatever it was away.

"Ow!" yelled the boa constrictor, sliding back behind the bush. "Nonnie! Sarah-Jane kicked me."

Grandma Patience had come out when she first heard the commotion. Now she looked into the bush. "Patience Elizabeth North. Are you hiding again?"

"I like to hide," said the bush.

"I know you do. But you come out of there right now. We talked about this before, young lady. It's wrong to make people worry about you. Now, come out of there and apologize to everyone."

To the others Grandma Patience said, "She's done this at home. Once we found her curled up in the kneehole of a desk. I thought I would lose my mind."

Patience did as she was told.

Then to Sarah-Jane she said, "You know, it would be easier to call me if I had a little name."

9

The Hundred-Year-Old House

It was not the best car trip they had ever been on.

For one thing, they were late getting started. And that made the grandmothers a little nervous.

They were late because of Patience hiding, of course. And because she got so dirty hiding it took forever to get her cleaned up.

On the way they stopped for lunch. That was good. But because they were running late, they had to skip dessert. That was bad. And it was all because of Patience.

But when Sarah-Jane saw the house, all other thoughts went clean out of her head.

"EXcellent!" said Titus beside her.

"Neat-O!" agreed Timothy.

"So cool!" said Sarah-Jane.

It was the biggest, fanciest house she had ever seen. It was the kind of house that made you want to wear long dresses and ruby necklaces and to ride in horse-drawn carriages.

She was dying to see inside, but she also felt a little scared.

Someone else must have been feeling the same way, because Sarah-Jane felt a little hand slide into hers.

Sarah-Jane looked down at the penny-red hair. Well, you couldn't stay mad forever. She gave the hand a little squeeze.

For once, Patience seemed at a loss for words.

But the grandmothers were not at a loss for words. They closed in for a little talk.

"All right, now. We're counting on you to be on your Best Behavior."

"Don't touch anything."

"And no running around."

"No loud noises."

"Patience, you stay with Sarah-Jane."

"Sarah-Jane, you *watch* her."

"Timothy and Titus, you help Sarah-Jane."

"Don't touch anything. Let's all just have a nice time."

Titus raised his hand as if he were in school. When Grandma called on him he said, "Does this mean we can't turn the place upside down looking for the ruby necklace?"

"We were looking forward to that," added Timothy wistfully.

"Oh, you guys," said Grandma with a laugh. "I can't take you anywhere." But she sounded kind of proud when she said it. Because she knew she really *could* take them anywhere.

Professor Brown greeted them at the front door. He seemed delighted to hear them gasp when they stepped into the hall.

Sarah-Jane had never seen anything like it. It was more like being in a church than a house.

The hall was paneled in rich, glowing wood. And high up in the corners were carved flowers and fruit and ribbons and birds. All carved by her own great-great-great-grandfather.

"Step into the library," said Professor Brown. "And I'll give you the guided tour. We haven't completed the entire house, yet. Some of the upstairs rooms are still empty. We'll finish them when we've raised more funds. Note the beautiful carving on the mantelpiece. Such workmanship. And over the mantelpiece you'll see a portrait of the original owners, who . . ."

"The ruby necklace!" cried Sarah-Jane before she could stop herself.

Professor Brown was delighted to repeat the story of the lost necklace that he had told Grandma Patience. But he was interrupted again. This time by Patience, who seemed to have gotten over her shyness.

"I HAVE TO GO POTTY!"

10

Upstairs Alone

"Oh, dear," murmured Grandma Patience. "I was afraid of this."

"I'll take her," volunteered Sarah-Jane.

"Oh, would you, dear?" said Grandma Patience. "That would be so helpful."

Professor Brown directed them to the staff room up the stairs and all the way down to the last room on the right.

"Come on, Patience," said Sarah-Jane. She felt incredibly grown-up. Doing a favor for the grandmothers. Being trusted to walk through the house on her own. Handling Patience without any trouble.

They found the washroom all right. But it seemed strange being up there all by themselves. The others seemed so far away. Rooms and rooms and rooms away.

Patience didn't want Sarah-Jane to come in with her. So Sarah-Jane waited outside in the hallway.

"Don't lock the door," she said.

"Why?"

"Because sometimes little kids lock themselves in and then they can't figure out how to unlock the door."

"I know," said Patience from the other side. "Because you know what? Once when I was little, we were at these people's house. And I locked myself in the bathroom. And you know what? The firemens had to come get me."

It sounded like another tall tale. But knowing Patience, it was probably true.

A sudden thought struck Sarah-Jane. "Patience Elizabeth North. Did you really have to go potty? Or did you just want to see the bathroom?"

"No, Sarah-Jane. I really have to go."

"Well, all right then. Just don't forget to wash your hands. And don't take all day."

"OK."

While she was waiting for Patience, Sarah-

Jane couldn't resist peeking in the rooms around her. Most of the rooms at this end of the hall were unfurnished.

Sarah-Jane tiptoed back toward the stairway. Here the rooms were all decorated. The beds were so high you needed a little stepstool to climb into them. And a couple of them even had a canopy. Sarah-Jane had always wanted a canopy. It would make you feel like a princess. Wait till Patience saw this.

Patience!

Sarah-Jane had actually forgotten why she was up there. Patience should have been out of the washroom by now.

Sarah-Jane turned and hurried back to the end of the hall. She tapped on the washroom door.

"Come on, Patience. I said not to take all day. They'll be wondering where we are."

There was no answer.

11

Missing

"Patience?"

Sarah-Jane opened the door and stepped into the washroom.

There was no one there.

The little bar of soap on the sink was all wet. And the paper towel in the waste paper basket was damp. So Patience had washed her hands as she had been told.

But where was she?

Then Sarah-Jane saw something she hadn't noticed before. There was another door in the washroom. And this door led to the staff room on the other side.

It had a kitchenette and a table and chairs. But no people today.

"Patience?"

Sarah-Jane was about to turn back when she noticed a door on the other side of the staff room. This door led to an empty bedroom beyond. Sarah-Jane glanced in. This room had a door that led to yet *another* room.

"Patience!"

Sarah-Jane looked around in dismay. Was Patience hiding again? Or had she just wandered off to peek in rooms as Sarah-Jane herself had? Either way, how would she ever find her? Sarah-Jane knew she had to get help.

She turned and fled back to the hallway, then down the hallway to the grand staircase. Even though she was worried about Patience, one part of her mind was imagining something else. Lady Sarah-Jane with her long dress billowing gracefully as she swept around the landing—

And slammed smack into Timothy and Titus.

"Ow!" said Timothy. "My cousin the linebacker. You know you're not supposed to be running, S-J."

"Shh!" said Sarah-Jane. "Just shut up and listen."

"You know you're not supposed to tell us to shut up, S-J," said Titus solemnly.

"Tim! Ti! Please! Quit kidding around! I need you to help me."

"OK, OK. What's up?"

Sarah-Jane took a deep breath. "I lost her."

"What?!"

"Patience. She's gone. She could be anywhere. You've got to help me find her. What's

Grandma going to say? I'm supposed to be watching her."

"It's all right, S-J," said Titus. "Grandma isn't worried or anything. The grown-ups are just talking and talking. Grandma just sent us to see if you'd gotten lost or something."

"Let's split up," suggested Timothy. "Don't worry, S-J. Wherever that kid can hide, the T.C.D.C. can find her."

But as it turned out, they didn't have to look very far.

They had just reached the top of the stairs when the washroom door burst open. Patience came running toward them.

She was grubby from head to toe. But her eyes were shining with excitement.

Before Sarah-Jane could scold her for running off and getting dirty, Patience spoke all in a rush. "You guys! You guys! Come see! Come see! The angels danced. I made them do it. I pulled on the clouds. And the angels danced!"

12

The Dancing Angels

"What's she talking about, S-J?" asked Timothy.

"Oh, who knows?" muttered Sarah-Jane. She was feeling relieved that Patience was safe but annoyed with her for running off. "We'd better go along with her. Otherwise we'll never get her back downstairs."

To Patience she said, "All right. Show us what you have to show us. But this had better not be another tall tale."

"It's not. I seed them with my own eyes, Sarah-Jane," said Patience earnestly.

"How did you get so sooty anyway?" Titus asked her. "What were you doing? Crawling around in a fireplace or something?"

"Yep," said Patience happily. As if this were

something people did all the time for fun.

Patience led them through the washroom, through the staff room, through the bedroom, and into the little room beyond.

"TAA-DAA!" she said. "See? I told you. Angels!"

The cousins stood and stared. They hadn't been expecting to see anything. Certainly not angels. But there they were. Beautiful, graceful angels. Carved all in a row into the mantelpiece. Carved by their own great-great-great-grandfather. It gave Sarah-Jane shivers—good shivers—just to think about it.

"Now, watch!" commanded Patience. "Watch me make them dance."

And before anyone could stop her, she darted into the fireplace. She was small enough to stand up under the mantel. She reached up and pulled on something.

And with a soft, scraping noise, the angels glided apart in a stately dance.

They left a dark open space in the middle of the mantel. Patience pulled on something again. With the same gentle dance, the angels glided together.

And it was as if the empty space had never been there.

13

The Angels' Secret

"Patience! How did you *do* that?" cried Timothy, Titus, and Sarah-Jane all together.

They rushed over to the fireplace and scooched down to look under the mantelpiece.

No one would have expected carvings under there where no one could see them. But their great-great-great-grandfather had taken the time to carve beautiful, puffy clouds there. If you looked really hard, you could see that one band of clouds stood out from the rest. They made a kind of handle or lever. And when you grasped it and pulled, the angel panel opened and closed.

A grown-up, who knew about the lever, could just reach under the mantel and pull it. Otherwise, you would never, ever guess.

So how had Patience found it?

She must have known what they were thinking, because she explained. "I finded it when I was hiding." She must have caught a look on Sarah-Jane's face, because she hurried on. "Then I saw all the pretty clouds. And I saw a cloud I could pull on. And I did. Because I wanted to see the angels dance."

As if on cue, all four of them said the rhyme together.

"Grasp the clouds by will or chance,
And you shall see the angels dance."

"Do you know what?" said Sarah-Jane. "Grandma always said she learned that rhyme from her grandmother."

"That's what Nonnie says, too," said Patience.

"Right," said Sarah-Jane. "Grandma and Nonnie had the same grandmother. And who was that? Long-ago Patience. I think Long-ago Patience made up the rhyme to tell about the mantelpiece. We didn't think you could *really* grasp a cloud. But Patience did. And she was right. We didn't think you could *really* see angels dance. But Patience did. And what do you know? She was right."

Patience nodded. "What do you know? I was right."

Of course, they each had to have a turn grasping the clouds to make the angels dance.

"A secret compartment!" said Titus. "This is just so incredibly excellent."

"You know what, though?" said Timothy. "We were so busy working the panel, we didn't even look inside."

14

The Discovery

"It's dark in that hole," said Patience.

"Never fear. Timothy's here!" said Timothy, and he pulled a tiny flashlight out of his pocket.

Titus ran to get a chair from the staff room.

"Me, me, me! Let *me* look!" said Patience.

The cousins glanced at one another. She *had* been the one to find the secret space. . . .

Titus put the chair in front of the fireplace for her to stand on. Sarah-Jane helped her to climb up. And Timothy held the flashlight.

"I see something!" cried Patience.

And without giving a thought to the dark or dirt or cobwebs, Patience reached into the hole.

Honestly! thought Sarah-Jane. *The kid has no fear.*

"I feel something!" cried Patience.

And she pulled out a metal box.

They knew the rule was: Don't touch anything.

But they couldn't help it.

The box wasn't locked. Inside the box there was another box. And inside that box was a soft velvet bag. And inside the bag was a ruby necklace.

They knew the rules were: Don't run. Don't yell.

But they couldn't help it.

15

Penny

It took a while—quite a while—to explain to the grown-ups just what had happened.

But when they understood it, they were absolutely thrilled.

"Imagine that, Grace!" exclaimed Grandma Patience. "We learned that little nursery rhyme, and we never knew that it meant anything. We just passed it along to our own grandchildren because we liked the sound of it. I think Sarah-Jane is right. I think Long-ago Patience made it up when she saw the work her father, Daniel, did on the mantelpiece. But maybe even she forgot what it was about."

Professor Brown said, "No one had any idea this secret compartment was there. Probably the only ones who ever knew about it were

Patience and her father and the original owners. And the owners were probably the only ones who knew that this is where they would hide the necklace. Until these children came along."

He looked at the cousins and Little Patience with amazement.

"Oh, you can depend on the T.C.D.C. all right," said Grandma Patience.

Professor Brown looked puzzled. "What's a 'teesy-deesy'?" he asked.

"It's letters," piped up Patience before anyone else could answer. "Capital B. Capital P. Capital V. Capital G. It stands for the Three Cousins Detective Club."

She tugged on Sarah-Jane's hand and looked up with big, pleading eyes. "Sarah-Jane. I helped find the necklace. Can't I please have a little name?"

All of a sudden, Sarah-Jane knew what she meant.

"Yes, Patience," she said. "I think it's time we gave you a little name."

Everyone looked to Sarah-Jane for an explanation.

"Patience wants a nickname. Just like when

we cousins call one another Tim, Ti, and S-J. Isn't that right, Patience?"

Patience nodded so hard they thought her head would fall off.

Sarah-Jane went on, "Patience wants a nickname to show she belongs to us cousins and to show that we belong to her."

Again Patience nodded.

"What's short for Patience?" asked Titus. "Pat?"

But Patience shook her head. "Pat is my teddy bear's name." She sounded surprised that he didn't already know that.

"How about initials?" suggested Timothy. "Patience Elizabeth North. P.E.N. Pen."

"A pen is something you write with," said Patience doubtfully.

"But not if you turn it into a girl's name," said Sarah-Jane. "Especially if the girl has hair the same color as a . . ."

"Penny!" said Timothy and Titus.

"Penny," repeated Patience. "Penny. Penny. Penny. Penny. Penny. *I'm* Penny!"

Later that day the grandmothers pulled

Sarah-Jane aside and thanked her for taking care of Patience.

"You are so patient with her!" exclaimed Grandma Patience.

Sarah-Jane couldn't believe her ears. "*Me? Patient?* Are you kidding?"

"Oh, you were wonderful," said Grandma Patience. "I love that child with all my heart. But she does drive me crazy sometimes."

"Me, too," said Sarah-Jane in a small voice.

The grandmothers laughed and hugged her.

Grandma said, "Being patient with people doesn't mean that they don't drive us crazy sometimes. It means treating people well even so."

Grandma Patience said, "I just hope looking after my little pumpkin wasn't too boring for you."

Sarah-Jane shook her head. "Nope! That's one thing you can say about Patience. She's *not* boring!"

The End

Series for Young Readers* From Bethany House Publishers

★ ★ ★

THE ADVENTURES OF CALLIE ANN

by Shannon Mason Leppard

Readers will giggle their way through the true-to-life escapades of Callie Ann Davies and her many North Carolina friends.

★ ★ ★

BACKPACK MYSTERIES

by Mary Carpenter Reid

This excitement-filled mystery series follows the mishaps and adventures of Steff and Paulie Larson as they strive to help often-eccentric relatives crack their toughest cases.

★ ★ ★

THE CUL-DE-SAC KIDS

by Beverly Lewis

Each story in this lighthearted series features the hilarious antics and predicaments of nine endearing boys and girls who live on Blossom Hill Lane.

★ ★ ★

RUBY SLIPPERS SCHOOL

by Stacy Towle Morgan

Join the fun as home-schoolers Hope and Annie Brown visit fascinating countries and meet inspiring Christians from around the world!

★ ★ ★

THREE COUSINS DETECTIVE CLUB®

by Elspeth Campbell Murphy

Famous detective cousins Timothy, Titus, and Sarah-Jane learn compelling Scripture-based truths while finding—and solving—intriguing mysteries.

* (ages 7–10)

9611